D0485589

NOVA IN
NEW YORK

MAY 2019

NOVA IN NEW YORK

Katherine Richards

ORCA BOOK PUBLISHERS

Copyright © 2019 Katherine Richards

All rights reserved. No part of this publication may be reproduced or transmitted in any form or by any means, electronic or mechanical, including photocopying, recording or by any information storage and retrieval system now known or to be invented, without permission in writing from the publisher.

Library and Archives Canada Cataloguing in Publication

Richards, Katherine, 1994–, author
Nova in New York / Katherine Richards.
(Orca limelights)

Issued in print and electronic formats.
ISBN 978-1-4598-2029-6 (softcover).—ISBN 978-1-4598-2030-2 (pdf).—
ISBN 978-1-4598-2031-9 (epub)

I. Title. II. Series: Orca limelights
PS8635.I269N69 2019   jc813'.6   c2018-904782-8
c2018-904783-6

First published in the United States, 2019
Library of Congress Control Number: 2018954164

Summary: In this high-interest novel for teen readers, Nova goes to New York for a summer dance program at the prestigious Joffrey Ballet School.

Orca Book Publishers is dedicated to preserving the environment and has printed this book on Forest Stewardship Council® certified paper.

Orca Book Publishers gratefully acknowledges the support for its publishing programs provided by the following agencies: the Government of Canada, the Canada Council for the Arts and the Province of British Columbia through the BC Arts Council and the Book Publishing Tax Credit.

Edited by Tanya Trafford
Cover design by Ella Collier
Cover photography by iStock.com/martinedoucet

ORCA BOOK PUBLISHERS
orcabook.com

Printed and bound in Canada.

22 21 20 19 • 4 3 2 1

For my parents. Thank you.

One

O n my last morning at home, the giant orange sun rose into the fiery sky. As I biked to Aunt Ivy's I could hear her words. *Red sky at night, sailors' delight, red sky in the morning, sailors take warning.* I couldn't shake the sense of dread that trickled down my spine. My palms stuck to the handlebars. Although it was still early, my skin was already damp from the heat. I turned off the highway and onto the gravel lane.

Aunt Ivy was sitting on the porch when I came through the gate. She held a mug against her chest. Her oxygen tank rested at her feet. Another mug sat on the table at her elbow. For me. "Coffee...too...much milk...no sugar."

She paused every few words to breathe. Her lungs had to work twice as hard as anyone else's.

I dropped my bike onto the grass and settled in beside her.

She asked, "You're...all packed? Passport? Pointe shoes? Toothbrush?"

"Three pairs of new pointe shoes with ribbons and elastics sewn on," I replied.

A few shallow breaths. "You'll love...New York. I went there before...you were...born... with your dad. It's got...such an...energy...to it— bursting with...skyscrapers...and people."

I sipped my coffee to avoid responding. I had auditioned for the summer intensive because that's what my ballet teachers expected of their advanced students. Two months of no training was too long. Muscles lost their strength, flexibility and precision in less. But I had not expected to get in. I kept waiting for excitement to settle in, the jitters of happiness. Girls fought for the chance to train with the renowned teachers at Joffrey Ballet School. But I just felt anxious.

Dad signed me up for ballet when I was seven. Since then he had often found Aunt Ivy and me dancing barefoot in her backyard, surrounded by flowers. She'd leave her oxygen tank on the step. Out on the grass, she'd raise her arms to her shoulders and twirl, head thrown back. I'd spin beside her.

"Do you feel that, Nova?" she'd ask. "Do you feel it?"

And there, with Aunt Ivy beside me, I always felt the bubbled joy in my chest. In those moments it felt like she didn't have cystic fibrosis. That she could do anything she wanted with her life. She seemed at her best when we spoke ballet-anything. Her breathing appeared less burdened, easier, fuller, *better.*

"Bug?" Aunt Ivy leaned toward me, bringing me back to the front porch. "New York? Are you...excited?"

I stirred my coffee, focusing on the swirling liquid in my mug. "Yeah, just nervous."

She settled back into her chair. "Perfectly... normal...but it's going...to be...wonderful...I can... feel it. I can't wait...to hear...all about it."

* * *

I left Aunt Ivy's at nine with a cucumber sandwich tucked in my basket. She wanted me to have a snack for the plane. She waited at the gate as I biked away. At the end of the lane I dropped one sneaker-clad foot on the pavement and looked back. She stood there, waving with both arms, her wrists crossing above her head. I blew her a kiss and then pedaled away.

At home my key grated in the lock, resisting. Cool air met me when I stepped inside.

"Nova? That you?" my dad replied, his voice muffled by the whir of the air conditioner. He always asked even though it was just the two of us.

"Just your friendly neighborhood burglar," I called out. Guilt made my stomach churn. My dad would be alone while I was in New York, wandering around a too-big house. He'd have no one to call out to when he got home from work. There would be no Sundays at the Grand River Raceway, making five-dollar bets. He'd have to go star searching by himself.

My dad stepped out of his office. His tie was loosely tied around his neck, and his sleeves were rolled to his elbows. A smudge of blue ink ran down his temple and mixed into his silver hair.

"You said goodbye to Ivy?"

"There's ink on your face." I tapped the side of my head. "Yeah, she said to call after you've dropped me at the airport."

"Right. Will do." He rubbed at the smudge. "Reminds me, I bought you something to eat on the plane..." He went back into his office and rummaged through his briefcase.

When he couldn't find what he was looking for, he began to search the room. "You excited?"

I leaned on the doorframe and avoided the question. "Are you sure you'll both be okay while I'm gone?"

He began to empty his jacket pockets. "Of course. I know you don't believe it, but Ivy and I can take care of ourselves."

I spotted a grocery bag on the floor and pulled out a deli sandwich. "Dad." I held it out. I didn't tell him Aunt Ivy had already made me one.

"Oh! There it is! New York will be amazing, and the school will be amazing. This is what you've always wanted, Nova." He pulled me in for a hug. "Don't second-guess yourself now."

I wrapped my arms around him in return.

He released me and headed to the front door, where I had stacked my luggage. "Now let's get you to the airport."

I followed him out. I wanted to believe his words. I wanted to believe that this summer program would be the best thing for me. But I wasn't sure about anything.

Two

New York made my ears ring. Pedestrians crossed against traffic lights, and cars honked at them. The constant noise and activity was overwhelming.

The buildings ran together as my cab zigzagged through the streets. An unending stream of people crowded the sidewalks. Women in pencil skirts and dangerously high stilettos, and men with slicked-back hair and tailored suits. Everyone was on their phone. Tourists were mixed in with the businesspeople. They wore oversized backpacks and carried extra-large bottles of water.

The cab suddenly swerved to the curb, and the driver clicked off the meter. "We're here," he announced.

I unfolded and counted out the American bills Dad had given me. The driver grabbed my bags out of the trunk, dropped them on the sidewalk and sped away.

I stood with my backpack slung over one shoulder and a suitcase clutched in each hand. I took another look around. I was in New York! The air stuck to my skin, and sweat gathered along my upper lip. I turned to face the building where I would be sleeping. It looked old, with pillars on either side of the door and big windows that curved on top. Like a picture from my history textbook.

I took a deep breath and tried to push down the memory of saying goodbye to Dad at the airport. *Just do your best, kiddo.* His hands had been stuffed into his pockets when I waved and disappeared through security. And the memory of Aunt Ivy by her gate, watching as I biked away. My throat tightened.

I glanced down at my watch: 2:01 PM. Nothing left to do but go inside.

The lobby had white-and-black checkerboard tiled floors. An overstuffed red couch sat along one wall. The other was lined with small, square mailboxes. A lady with short gray hair and glasses perched on her nose sat behind the desk.

I walked up to her. A brass nameplate by her computer said *Miss Reed*. "Nova Abbott, for the pre-professional program?" I said. Nerves trickled into my voice.

The high ceilings amplified the clatter of her keyboard as she typed. She glanced up after a final click. "Nova. Welcome." She collected pages from a whirring printer and a key from the wall. "You are in room 314. Stairs are just to your left. Here's your key." She held up a silver key and slid it across the desk to me. "And your meal-plan card for breakfast and dinner. Meals are in the cafeteria just around the corner." She leaned forward and pointed to the hall on my right.

I slipped the card and key into my pocket. "Right. Thanks."

She gave me a businesslike nod before returning her gaze to her monitor. "Enjoy your stay. Let us know if you need anything."

There was no elevator. I dragged my suit-cases up the stairs to the third floor. All the doors along the hallway were open. The space hummed with excitement. As I made my way down the hall I could see girls unpacking stuffed suitcases, making their beds and putting up pictures of friends and family from home.

Like all the other rooms, mine had beige walls and a single window covered with a brown floor-to-ceiling curtain. There were two dressers, plus metal-frame bunk beds pushed into a corner. I threw my backpack on the top bunk and climbed up the ladder. Sitting cross-legged on the bed, I pulled Aunt Ivy's sandwich from my bag. The taste of cucumber and creamy ranch dressing spread over my tongue. My favorite. Aunt Ivy was one of the people who knew me best.

A girl dragging three large pink suitcases came into the room. Her blond hair was pulled back into a high ponytail and tied with a bright pink scrunchie. A small gold stud sparkled in her turned-up nose. "Hi, I'm Immy—that's Immy with two *m*'s and a *y*. I'm your roommate!"

I swallowed the bite of sandwich still in my mouth. Her voice was loud and high pitched. "Nova," I said.

Immy tilted her head to the side. "Like the star?"

"Yeah. My dad's really into astronomy." If there was one fact about Oliver Abbott, that was it. Every weekend, no matter the weather, Dad and I went star searching. Armed with our star map, we'd hike away from the light until it was just us and the darkness. We often ended up at the quarry. We would lie back on the rocky cliffs, enjoying the gentle sound of the water hitting the cliff walls below us, like the meteors that streaked across the sky, Dad said that I was an unexpected brightness in his life. My throat tightened again.

Immy opened her luggage and began to sort her clothes into piles. It looked like everything she owned was in varying shades of pink. "So how long have you been dancing?"

"Ten years, since I was seven. You?"

She raised her eyebrows in disbelief. "Seven? That's late, isn't it?" Without waiting for an answer, she plowed on. "It is, really. I started just after my third birthday. Jazz, tap, ballet, contemporary, you name it. My teacher says it's all about diversity—pushing your abilities so you can be a more expressive dancer." She placed clothes into the dresser. "Your body is your instrument."

"Right. Well, I guess I'm really more of a ballet girl." I ate the last bite of my sandwich and rolled the plastic wrap between my palms.

Immy paused in her unpacking and turned to me. "You *only* do ballet?" she asked.

I nodded. It wasn't that big a deal.

"How are you going to get into a company and become a soloist like that?" She stood with her hands on her hips, looking up at me. "Do you have a five-year plan for how you're going to make it? My mom and I revise mine every August based on my progress." Immy returned to her suitcases and dug out another load of pink leotards.

"Umm...I haven't decided yet if I want to dance professionally."

Immy moved back to the dresser. "Well then, you're obviously in the wrong place. Because we're all here to make it. If you're not, then you'll get left behind."

Three

My alarm rang at seven thirty the next morning. I groaned. Immy had snored the whole night. Deep, chest-rumbling snores that could not be muffled by pillows. I had barely slept. It was all I could do to stay awake at the studio as we waited for the teacher to arrive. I stretched in center splits and rested my forehead against the floor.

Around me the eleven other girls in the program warmed up for class too. Some did pliés at the barre, their feet pressed into perfect turn-outs with each bend of their legs. Others swung their legs back and forth to warm up their hips. At the front of the studio Immy was pinning her hair into a bun. I had chosen my spot carefully, making sure we were separated by as many girls as possible.

"Ladies!" A man breezed through the door with three loud claps. I sat up so I could see him better. He had closely buzzed black hair. His ballet slippers were well worn along the toes. I noticed a puckered scar around his kneecap. "I'm Isaac, one of your instructors. Now, because it's a pre-professional program, and we only have two weeks, classes will move quickly. You will be treated like professional dancers. And we expect you to behave like committed professionals." He picked up the remote for the music system. "Any questions?"

No one raised their hand.

"All right. Let's get started. We'll begin with pliés."

Isaac did not waste any time. He demonstrated the first exercise once, with shorthand movements to show each step. Then he signaled us to prepare to dance it to music. "I want you to focus on your posture throughout the exercise. Always start your class the way you intend to go on. Keep your shoulders back, your chest open and your ab muscles engaged. We'll go right into the other side after this one." He cued the music. "And, five, six, seven, eight."

He walked up and down the row throughout the exercise, adjusting a girl's turnout here, an arm placement there, or the angle of someone's head and the set of her shoulders.

I focused on my plié and tried not to track his progress down the barre toward me. Heels together and toes pointing out in first position. Bend my knees slowly in each plié. Take up the full count with each bend and stretch. I was standing in second position when Isaac reached me. My right arm was stretched out like I was waiting for a hug.

He pressed down on my arm. "Name?"

"Nova."

"Hold your arm, Nova." He pressed down on my bicep again, and my arm dropped. "Resist my hand." I tightened my muscles and resisted. He nodded and moved on. "Engage your muscles, girls! You're not relaxing on the beach, you're dancing!"

By the end of the first exercise, sweat rolled over my temples. After clicking off the music, Isaac immediately demonstrated tendus, his foot moving out to a stunning point. "Make sure you're going through your foot, like you're pushing through gum, to get it fully stretched in front of you. Ready? Prepare." He started the music again.

We went back and forth, Isaac demonstrating the steps and us performing them. It was almost like a game of tag. Sometimes he stopped an exercise and gave corrections before getting us to start it again from the top. His leg was perfectly in line with his shoulders when he demonstrated an arabesque to the back.

We did center work in shifts, two groups of six. My balance was off from the start. I almost fell over when I moved into a forward bend.

"Nova, focus! Hold your ab muscles!" Isaac kept calling.

When we did pirouettes, I could barely make a single turn. My foot seemed to stick to the floor, my arms lagged behind my body as I spun around, and I finished each turn dizzy. Isaac came over to me and held his hands palms up. I rested my hands in his.

He gestured with his chin. "Rise." I rose onto my demi-pointe and raised my right leg into a retiré, so my legs looked like a numeral four. "Focus. You're not moving as a single unit. Coordinate each individual movement in your body so that everything happens at once. Every muscle is working toward the same goal. Hold your abdominals so you have more stability. Keep your shoulders down and whip your head around faster in your spot so you don't get dizzy. Find the front of the room as soon as you can. You're inclining your head, and it's throwing your balance off."

Isaac dropped his hands. I stayed in my retiré and tried to coordinate my muscles to follow his instructions. When I fell out of the position again, I caught myself with the leg that had previously been lifted. Reset. Pirouette.

Isaac was watching when I landed, his arms folded across his chest. "Better. You're leaning back though. Next group." He cued the music for the other group of girls.

I went to the barre and practiced pulling my legs underneath me in a quick rise. Frustration made me tense. I had done countless pirouettes— in classes, performances, across Aunt Ivy's lawn. But my coordination just wasn't working today.

My head felt like it was stuffed with cotton. My thoughts were clouded, and I couldn't focus on the basic steps, my technique or Isaac's corrections. *Focus.* Abdominals engaged, shoulders down, neck relaxed.

"Spot your head, Immy," I heard Isaac call from the front. I turned to watch the other group. The girls all looked like ballerinas in a jewelry box, rotating effortlessly on their legs. All they needed were pointe shoes and tutus and they could be in a performance.

Isaac called, "Good, Harriet! Keep your foot pointed in the turn." She had just landed a perfect triple. Her legs looked a mile long. Sweat dotted her hairline, but unlike most of us, unlike me, Harriet's bodysuit remained dry. Her long neck screamed Odette from *Swan Lake.*

I pulled my soaked leotard away from my body for a release from the clingy, hot fabric. Isaac switched CDs.

"All right, class. Now we'll do some turns across the floor. Everyone pair up."

The room filled with whispers and the sound of shuffling feet as we made our way to the back corner. We were all making eye contact with each other to claim partners. I took a step closer to the girl on my left.

"I'm Nova."

"Beth." She adjusted her leotard strap. Beth had dark skin and tight curls pulled into a fluffy bun. She wore a brace on her left knee, and electric green tape streaked across her back. "This studio seriously needs air-conditioning."

Isaac clapped his hands. "Six posé pirouettes, chaîné, chaîné, chaîné, chaîné, arabesque." He mimed each movement with his hands. One hand held at the elbow of his other arm to show our posé turns. For chaîné turns he held one finger up and flicked his wrists. I was never any good at chaînés. They were just tight, consecutive turns, but they always made me dizzy.

The girls going before me were all graceful, with long legs and pointed feet. They could have been flying across the stage. When my turn came I felt like the Ugly Duckling. My weight was still too far back, and I kept falling out of my balance.

Isaac called, "Nova, adjust your placement!"

I lifted from my waist, imagining I could touch the Milky Way. It helped me add half a turn before my left foot slipped from my right knee again. My turns were loose and slow compared to the tight spirals of the other girls. It felt like I shouldn't be there.

Four

"This heat is killing me." Beth draped herself over the barre. The fans that hung in the corners of the studio were already on full, but circulating the air did little to dull the humidity. It was inescapable. We were now on day three. Beth and I had become fast friends, meeting for breakfast in the morning and spending all our time together outside class.

I stood beside her, stretching my hamstrings. My stomach was pressed against my legs, and my palms were flat on the floor. "You get used to it," I said, my voice muffled. That was a lie. All I wanted to do was jump into the crystal-blue water at the quarry.

"I'd move if Vancouver got like this in the summer." Her voice came out in a groan. "It's too hot to think, let alone dance."

Isaac walked past us just then. "Glad to hear your enthusiasm for class, Beth. On that note, let's get the day started with some pliés. I want to focus on jumps today, so we'll do a quick barre."

Immy squealed. "I *love* jumps—they're my specialty." She was pretending to speak to Harriet, Immy's new shadow, but spoke loud enough for the entire studio to hear. Harriet giggled. Beth rolled her eyes at me and turned to face the front of the studio.

Isaac clapped for attention. "Ladies, settle down. Let's all focus. We'll start with the same plié exercise as yesterday. Remember to use all the counts—really warm up your muscles." He started the music. "And begin."

The exercises weren't as bad as on that first day, but they were still hard. I was relieved when Isaac called. "Grab a drink and then we'll move on." He changed the CD while we broke out of our lines to get our water bottles.

We started with changements, small jumps where you switch which foot is in front. "Let's do thirty-two to warm up." Heat surged over my skin with each jump, landing in plié, engaging my thighs to get me back into the air. My muscles already felt defeated by the heat and the strain. The water break had not been enough, and I could feel the sweat on my upper lip. In Aunt Ivy's backyard we would have stopped dancing and switched to sipping tart lemonade in the shade.

"*Jump*, Nova! You're barely leaving the ground." The exasperation in Isaac's voice brought me back to the studio, the music muffled by the noise of the fans. "Use your feet to push off the ground, girls!"

I counted the jumps in my head—eighteen, nineteen, twenty...Deep plié, roll through the feet, point toes in the air. Twenty-six, twenty-seven, twenty-eight...

"Keep your weight over your toes when you plié, girls, weight *forward!*" Isaac yelled. "I shouldn't be able to hear you! You sound like a stampede of elephants when you land!"

Weight forward, roll through the foot, plié, plié, plié. Lemonade, lemonade, lemonade. Thirty, thirty-one, thirty-two.

Isaac paused the music. "Again," his voice flat.

One, two, three, four, five. Point, point, point. Arms held long and oval, elbows rounded, fingers away from the thighs. For bras bas back home, my teacher, Miss Lilly, had once made us each hold a CD case for an entire class. She wanted to make sure our hands weren't too far apart. Aunt Ivy had laughed when I told her that, her oxygen-cart wheels squeaking as we walked to the car.

Thirty, thirty-one, thirty-two. Done. I bent over, my hands braced on my knees. I couldn't catch my breath. Sweat ran down my chest and into my leotard, making the material stick to my skin.

Isaac wasted no time announcing the next exercise. "To the corner, ladies. We'll do a zigzag of grand jetés across the floor, one at a time."

Harriet went first, then Immy. I noticed her split was not quite flat in the air. I took my position behind Beth. I stepped into the zigzag, focused on keeping my weight forward so I'd be able to jump high enough. Shoulders down and jeté. I unfolded my right leg in front and kept my left leg straight in the back. I glanced into the mirror. A flat split, good height.

"Nice, Nova! Just lower your right arm to your eyebrow," said Isaac. Relief made my chest loosen. My breaths seemed to come easier, even with the jumps. Finally, finally, a compliment. Isaac's praise made me feel like I really could touch the Milky Way. My final jump was high and light and almost easy, almost natural. When I finished I ran to join the line along the barre. Beth gave me a high five.

Isaac glanced at the clock. "We'll do fouettés to finish, ladies. Groups of two in the center, please."

I groaned. I wasn't a fan of this type of turn. It was so hard to coordinate my legs, arms and head while turning and turning. "This will be a disaster," I mumbled to Beth. Just when I had finally got some praise from Isaac.

Immy and Harriet peeled off from the barre to go first. Isaac played the music.

Beth gave me a small hip check. "Just relax. You can do it."

"Good, Immy," Isaac called. "Remember to focus your eyes on one spot at the front."

I tilted my head toward my shoulder to stretch the muscles of my neck. They felt tight with tension and nerves. The next pair of girls went. Their turns were quick. I counted them—fifteen, sixteen, seventeen... Eighteen before one of the girls lost her balance and fell out. She started again.

Beth and I moved into the center and prepared. I pliéd and did a single pirouette to start. Then I extended my right leg to the front and out to the side in a single motion, snapping it back into my knee so I turned. One down. Again. I focused on whipping my head around in each turn. If I got dizzy, then all was lost.

"You're leaning to the right, Nova," said Isaac. I adjusted my weight.

"Good, Beth. Higher arm in second position."

The most fouettés I managed was nine in a row. Isaac had not asked for a set number of turns. He just let the music play. Each time one of us fell over, we started again.

My turns on the other side were even worse. I barely did four in a row. I couldn't seem to get my legs and arms and head to work together. When the music finally stopped I wiped the sweat from my forehead and headed back to the barre.

As I walked past Isaac he said, "You really need to work on those, Nova."

The last two girls went. Issac turned off the music and said, "Thanks for class today ladies." To me, "Nova, can you stay behind for a moment?"

"I'll meet you back at the dorm," Beth whispered.

Isaac waited until all the other girls had left, their pointe shoes slung over their shoulders as they filed out.

He set the remote down on the piano. "Nova, you beat out thousands of others to get a spot in this program," he said quietly. "I watched your audition tape. I know what you can do. You're a strong dancer—but I'm having a hard time seeing that in class. I think it's time for you to decide if you really want to be here. Right now it's just not there."

I tightened my grasp on my pointe shoes. "Okay," I croaked.

"I know you have it in you—I just have to see it." His voice was gentle. "Now go rest up."

I didn't have a response for him. I moved toward the door. My throat was tight with tears and I blinked to clear my eyes. My bare feet squeaking against the hardwood was the only sound in the studio. I slipped into my flip-flops and threw on my T-shirt, not bothering with pants. I took deep breaths as I made my way down the stairs and out into the lobby. The security guard nodded at me from behind her desk. I knew my dancing in class hadn't been enough—but hearing it said out loud was brutal. Especially from someone as talented as Isaac.

The city hum greeted me as I stepped out of the building. Everyone had somewhere to be, someone to meet. I let them jostle solitary me from side to side all the way back to the dorm. I didn't have the energy to resist.

My phone rang as I climbed the stairs to my floor. A picture of Aunt Ivy popped up on the screen. She was kneeling in front of a bed of sweet peas, oxygen tank almost hidden by the grass.

I swiped to answer the call. "Hey."

"Bug! Your dad and I...are getting...worried... not hearing...from you...in so long. I want all... the details—New York...classes...the other girls. Don't hold...back." A loud rustle sounded in the speaker. "Sorry...Bug...adjusting...my oxygen. Now...New York."

"Right." I focused on the gloss of the tiles along the stairs so I didn't slip. With each step my sandal slapped against a blister on the bottom of my foot. "It's great. Hard. All the other girls are really good. Some are doing quads in pirouettes. And the instructors are all amazing." I tried to sound enthusiastic. "I'm learning a lot."

I reached my room and unlocked the door. I was really hoping Immy and Harriet were not inside—I could not face them right now. The room was empty. Good, they were out.

"You sure...you're okay? You sound...off."

"Just tired. How are you?" Aunt Ivy's breaths sounded shallower than usual. "And Dad?"

"Oh...chugging...along. Missing you."

"Miss you too." Saying it out loud brought a sour taste to my mouth.

Someone knocked on the door. Beth popped her head into the room. "Novaaaaaaa—" She stopped when I turned around to face her, phone pressed to my ear. *Sorry*, she mouthed.

Seeing her pulled me back to New York. Horns honked outside, and cars sped by. My panic started to settle and blur at the edges.

I swallowed instead of telling Aunt Ivy what Isaac had said.

"One second, Aunt Ivy." I took the phone away from my ear.

"When you're done, do you want to go explore the city?" Beth asked.

"Yes. *Yes*," I said. I needed to get out of my head—away from my doubts about what I was actually doing here.

Five

This time I embraced the chaos of New York. It felt good to be tossed back and forth between people. I was so busy staying close to Beth that I couldn't overthink.

Totally used to the big city, Beth powered through the crowds. Her hand firmly grasped mine to make sure I wasn't left behind. Every so often she stopped to look at the map on her phone. When she did, I took a moment to tip my head back and squint against the sun. I stared at the pillars and brick and glass that made up this city.

Suddenly, after a quick right turn, Beth threw open her arms. "Here we are! *Broadway.*"

It looked like any other street to me. Maybe busier. The sidewalks were packed. Cars crawled forward, honking at people crossing in front of them.

Beth could tell by my face that I was not impressed with it. She sighed and linked her arm through mine. "How do you know *nothing* about New York? This is the longest street in Manhattan, famous for its theater district. And great shopping!"

Billboards flashed, and color burst from every direction. I turned slowly, trying to take it all in.

Beth skipped with excitement. "C'mon!" she cried, pulling me along.

We went into every clothing store we passed and tried on outfit after outfit. We couldn't afford any of them. Crop tops with bell sleeves paired with pleated skirts patterned with flowers, and sandals with three-inch platforms. Dresses that reached the floor, with plunging backs, and others with laces down the front. Aunt Ivy would have called them *indecent*. Hats with brims that flopped over our faces, and sunglasses that hid our eyebrows.

After an extra-long session at Bloomingdale's, Beth asked, "You hungry?"

"Donuts?"

"Yes, please!" She checked her phone as we made our way to the front of the store. "There's a donut shop about twenty minutes—this way." She did a hard left when we pushed through the doors, and the city crowd swallowed her up. All I could see were her curls, springing with each step. As I ran to catch up, a store's window display caught my eye.

"Beth? Beth!" She turned, and I pointed behind me. "Can we just check out that store real quick?"

It was small, no more than ten feet wide, and displays of jewelry lined each wall. Aunt Ivy loved jewelry. She collected new pieces from markets wherever she went. Something from New York would be the perfect surprise. Stones of every color were set into different metals in delicate patterns. I walked along the shelves, pausing at each new display. Light danced off the polished stones. I stopped at a necklace strung with garnets, each sandwiched between silver beads that set off the stone's burgundy glow. It screamed Aunt Ivy.

"Excuse me?" I said. The girl behind the display case looked up. She put her book down and came over. "How much is that one?"

She opened the case and glanced at the price tag. "Eighty-three eighty."

Beth peered over my shoulder. "Nice! Are you going to buy it?"

I converted to Canadian dollars in my head. "I'll think about it."

*   *   *

We ate our donuts while we walked through Central Park. "That may have been the best thing I've ever eaten," Beth said, wiping her face and hands on a napkin.

"Yeah. I'll dream about that Red Velvet donut tonight." My donut was so good it almost made me want to stay in New York and the program just so I could have more.

We settled on the grass in a patch of sun. Along the bank of the lake, toddlers chased waddling ducks. Couples holding hands walked along the path. Runners and cyclists made their way around them.

"So what did Isaac say?" Beth asked.

I was grateful that she had waited until now to ask. Isaac's disappointment almost felt bearable under the sun with the donut's icing still sweet in my mouth. I didn't look at her when I answered. "He said I needed to step up my dancing or leave. But he also reminded me that I had made it into the program for a reason. So there's that."

Beth turned on her stomach and squinted up at me. "Most of the time in class I'm thinking about how it's so hot I'm about to fall over. And then somewhere in there dancing happens."

"The dancing just doesn't seem to happen for me."

"You have to get out of your head. Stop thinking about Immy and Harriet. Or Immy's grand plans for international ballet domination." Her phone rang. "Shoot," she said as she glanced at the screen, "it's my parents. I forgot I said we could talk today. I might be a while. You okay if I meet you back at the dorm?"

No. No, no, no, no, no. Out loud I said, "Yeah, sure." I stood, brushing grass off my shorts.

"Hello? Yeah, hey, Mom."

Beth got up, and we walked to the park

entrance. Beth *hmm*ed an occasional agreement to whatever her mom was saying on the other end.

"Just a sec, Mom." She looked at me with concern. "You sure you'll be okay getting back?"

"I'll be fine." I shooed her away.

"Don't forget to buy that necklace!" she yelled over her shoulder before she turned away and was swallowed by the crowd.

I stood there alone, taking in the buzz of traffic and people rushing to their next stop.

Deep breath. I can do this.

And then my phone's screen went dark.

Six

I needed a map. Panic fluttered in my stomach and I could hear my pulse in my ears. I didn't know the way back to the dorm. I had never been good with directions. Finding my way in the streets of the small town where I'd grown up was second nature. Biking to the quarry under the quiet night sky with Dad. Running errands into town with Aunt Ivy. The short trip between the ballet studio and home. I had always known these routes. And when we traveled, Dad acted as tour guide and I only had to follow.

I'd been too busy looking around at the buildings to notice which streets Beth and I had taken. Beth had been so sure of herself that I'd thought I didn't need to pay attention. I had read somewhere that there are more than eight million people in New York City. Eight million people not counting the tourists taking in the sights or businesspeople in town for important, high-powered meetings. *Eight million.*

I took a deep breath and thought of Aunt Ivy dropping me off for my first ballet lesson. My hair had been too short to pull into a bun. Instead, Aunt Ivy had clipped it back with randomly placed barrettes. And no matter how many times I pulled up my little pink ballet socks, they wouldn't stay put. They'd fall back down and pool around my ankles. I'd been too nervous to go into the class. Aunt Ivy had sat beside me on the steps of the studio, her head tilted as she listened to the music floating through the door.

After a few songs she had turned to me and said, "Bug, waiting is not making it any easier. You just have to get in there and start."

Waiting was not making this any easier—or making me any less lost. I took one more deep breath, and then I started.

*   *   *

With over eight million people to choose from, there had to be someone who could give me directions. I chose a couple of obvious tourists wearing sensible walking shoes and sun hats. They had a big map I could look at to find my way.

I repeated the directions we had traced out on their map over and over so I wouldn't forget. Left on Central Park Way, right on West 86th, continue until Broadway. *No problem. I've got this.* As I started to relax a bit, I found myself peering into the shop windows as I passed.

It was too hot. On 86th I stopped to buy an iced coffee from a café with flowerpots on its patio. As I sipped I moved between store awnings to avoid the sun. Condensation dripped down the sides of the plastic cup and onto my feet. I slipped through the doorway of a small shop that had air conditioning.

Racks of clothes were staggered throughout. A golden retriever dozed in front of a fan in the corner. Beside the only mirror, jewelry hung on a rack made of pipes. A sign on the display read *Handmade by Essi*. I twirled the display of bracelets, necklaces and rings. The various gems were set in geometric patterns with swirls of coiled wire.

The man behind the counter was making a necklace. He held a pair of needle-nose pliers in his hand and was studying the mixture of beads and wire spread on the counter in front of him. He glanced up. "Let me know if I can help you find anything."

A silver ring with a light-blue stone at its center caught my eye. The delicate series of swirled knots surrounding it didn't seem to have a beginning or end.

"It's based off an endless knot."

His voice startled me. The man—Essi, I assumed—looked at me through chunky black glasses. "The ring you're holding." He pointed with the pliers. "The design is loosely based on the Celtic love knot."

"It's beautiful." I turned the ring back and forth, catching the light. The blue was so pale that at certain angles it looked colorless, blending into the silver that surrounded it.

"The stone is an aquamarine."

I continued to turn the ring, watching the color drain and reappear. This was Aunt Ivy's ring. I set it on the counter. "I'll take it."

The sun was just visible between the buildings when I left the store with a small paper bag. I took my time now, letting my head drift back up to admire the reflections in the skyscraper windows. *The buildings bring the sky to earth with their reflections*, Aunt Ivy had said. I felt like I was starting to understand what she meant. When I reached the steps of my dorm, I realized my panic had faded.

Maybe, just maybe, I could do this.

Seven

The next morning I knocked on the studio door before class started and looked inside. My instructor stood at the stereo, putting CDs into the disc player.

"Isaac?" I moved inside, shutting the door behind me.

He turned. "Nova. How can I help?"

"I was wondering if I could use the studio after hours to practice."

He frowned. "Well, there are some logistical issues to work out—keys and such—but I think we can make it work. Let me see what I can do."

"Perfect." I sighed, relieved. "Thank you." I had been prepared for a flat-out no and knew I would have to figure something else out if I couldn't use the studio. Yesterday afternoon's adventure had filled me with resolve. I was determined to take full advantage of this opportunity.

The other girls started to come in. I went to my spot at the barre to warm up and stretch. Beth slipped in beside me. She had blue tape along her back today that went with her navy bodysuit. A matching scrunchie held her bun in place.

Isaac said, "It's pointe day, girls. Get your shoes on now, please."

Immy raised her hand. Beth glanced over her shoulder at me and rolled her eyes. *Classic Immy.*

"Yes, Immy?" Isaac said.

"I'm just wondering if we can focus on pirouettes today—they are so important for soloists."

"We'll see how it goes. In the meantime, shoes on."

We all settled on the floor. The clatter of pointe shoes echoed through the studio. "She really is a piece of work," said Beth, padding her toes with lamb's wool. "*Soloists* need to have perfect pirouettes. Come on."

"Well, she's got a goal. You have to give her credit for that." I slipped my foot into my pointe shoe and began tying the ribbons.

"We all have goals," said Beth. "We don't all rub them in other people's faces."

"True." Immy was annoying, but I wasn't going to let it affect me. My newfound determination was still strong. Isaac was right. I had made it into the program. I was here for a reason. And maybe tonight I would be able to practice without anyone judging.

On to the next pointe shoe. The shoe already felt confining, and it pressed my toes together. My feet must be swollen from the heat. I nudged Beth. "Hey, we'll get there. I have a good feeling about this."

Class was hard but I felt good after. I drank the last of my water as we filed out of the studio.

"Nova! A word," Isaac called.

Beth shot me a curious look as I changed direction.

"I talked to the building security guard, and she is willing to let you in and then lock the studio after," said Isaac.

"Oh, thank you. That's perfect."

"Why don't we go down to the lobby now, and I'll introduce you two." Isaac set down the remote and headed for the door. I readjusted my grip on my pointe shoes as I followed him out. *Let the rehearsals begin.*

Eight

A single light was on in the far corner of the studio when I came back later that evening. The floors creaked under my steps. The smell of rosin, the stuff we rub on our pointe shoes, lingered in the air and made the studio smell like evergreens. I clicked the stereo on. The CDs clicked as they changed. Soon a soft serenade of piano music drifted from the speakers.

I walked a circuit of the studio, swinging my arms and then holding each in turn across my body, stretching and warming up joint by joint. After that I went to the barre. The wood was smooth under my fingertips, cool, calming. I did slow rises, rolling my neck. My toes and ankles popped.

Pliés. I bent my knees until my heels began to creep off the floor. Stretched my legs. And again. I let my head follow my arm without worrying about whether my movements were perfect.

Each exercise rolled into the next. I was constantly in motion, fluid, *dancing*. In class I was focused on the little details that went into each step. But here, alone, it was just me and the movements.

I moved to the corner for pirouettes. I let my steps travel across the floor. I didn't have to worry about getting in the way of others or watch how the other girls did their turns. *Weight on the front foot, knees bent, neck relaxed. Whip my head around to find my spot.* Double pirouette landed. Again and again and again I practiced my pirouettes. Pirouettes in attitude, leg raised behind me and bent at the knee. Pirouettes from lunge. Pirouettes from the corner. Pirouettes in a circle around the room. Each turn felt natural, weightless, simple.

Without Isaac's sharp, ever-present eye and Immy's judgment, I wasn't self-conscious. I was only the pull of muscles and the push of feet against the floor and turns that *spun*.

Aunt Ivy had taken Dad and me to see *Swan Lake* for my eighth birthday. I had worn my favorite purple dress and socks with frills around the ankles. We had sat in the first balcony of the theater. The ballerinas glided across the stage, weightless, their feet fluttering like butterfly wings. I imagined that's what walking on water would look like. The swans had moved as one, sixteen pairs of pointe shoes rapping out the same rhythm in their flurry of tulle. Aunt Ivy had swayed in her seat beside me, her head moving in time with the steps of the dancers, her upper body dancing along.

At intermission Aunt Ivy had returned from the bar with three flutes of sparkling apple juice. The golden liquid had bubbled along the rims of the glasses. "For the birthday girl." She'd handed one to me and the other to Dad and then tipped her glass against mine. "To eight years. Cheers."

The bubbles had fizzed against my throat when I sipped it, and the sweetness of apple had spread over my tongue. I'd hummed to myself, tapping my toes like I was in dance class and weaving around Aunt Ivy and Dad while they talked.

"The Swan Princess seems sad," I'd said, interrupting.

"She's cursed to turn into a swan every day," Aunt Ivy replied. "She's only a girl at night."

Another sip as I contemplated. "That's sad."

Aunt Ivy had smoothed a curl from my cheek. "That's why she's dancing."

On the way home I'd imagined the passing cars were swans. "How do ballerinas walk on their toes?" I'd asked from the back seat.

"Lots of practice," Aunt Ivy responded.

"And a high tolerance for pain," Dad added.

I'd dozed off after that, lulled to sleep by their voices. Next thing I knew, Dad was carrying me into the house.

"Dad?" I'd mumbled, curling into his chest.

"Mmm?" His hum had vibrated through my cheek.

"I think I might want to walk on my toes too."

"Then you will."

And now, in the dark studio, as sweat dripped down my spine, I remembered that feeling. My steps went beyond technique. It was only me and the music and the movements, dancing like a swan princess.

Nine

I called Aunt Ivy for the third time that night while I climbed the stairs to my room. Still nothing. Straight to voice mail at Dad's number too. I chewed my lip. She hadn't been due for any doctor's appointments when I left.

"Finally!"

I glanced up from my phone to see Beth at the top of the stairs, her arms in the air.

"I've been looking *everywhere* for you."

I slid my phone into my pocket. "You're being dramatic."

"Since dinner. I've been looking for you since dinner. Where have you been?"

I realized there was no way I could keep my new plan a secret. "I asked Isaac if I could practice in the studio after hours." I rolled my shoulders back to ease my tired muscles.

"No way! Can I come with you next time?" She fell into step with me on the way to my room.

"Of course." It would be nice to have some company.

*   *   *

"I can't move." We were in the studio the next morning. I lay on the floor beside Beth. "Even rolling over to turn off my alarm hurt."

Beth leaned forward in her center-splits stretch, resting her cheek against the hardwood. "You said that at breakfast."

"And you're rubbing in your flexibility."

"Girls!" A woman crossed the studio, clapping for attention. "I am Miss Natalia, and I will be leading class today." She spoke with a thick Russian accent. "Now, pliés." Three quick claps.

Where was Isaac?

Miss Natalia's hair was knotted in a tight French twist. She wore several thin gold bracelets that jingled when she moved. She didn't demonstrate exercises like Isaac did but only said the steps while miming them with her hands.

She shouted over the music. "Imagine you are an accordion! You never stop moving, never sit in a plié." Miss Natalia paced up and down the row of dancers. Occasionally she'd step closer to a girl to examine placement.

When the music finished she went back to the stereo and restarted the same song. "Again." She played the same piece of music.

Again, again, again was her refrain throughout the class. At one point I found myself holding her hands in the center of the room, balanced on my right leg with my left bent behind me at the knee. I ignored my tired and sore muscles to maintain the position. I could do this. I *would* do this.

She dropped one of my hands and pushed each shoulder back. "You're leaning forward. You need to lift." My muscles strained with the effort and my foot cramped. "Now." She took a step back and released my other hand. I fought to keep my back up and my leg high, taking care that my knee didn't droop. She tilted her head and nodded before turning away. "Why are none of you other girls practicing? I am not correcting..." She turned and raised her eyebrows at me.

"Nova," I said.

"Nova for my own amusement." She snapped her fingers. "Practice."

Pirouettes for the fourth time across the floor. Immy and Harriet first. Harriet's diagonal was too steep, and she crashed into Immy before the first turn. We were all starting to show signs of fatigue. My turn. My muscles and joints seemed to know what was coming and began to protest. *Weight forward, peel the foot off the floor. Choose a spot on the wall, whip the head around in each turn. One turn, two turn, three.* Excitement shimmied down my spine when I landed my triple. Miss Natalia eyed me for a moment as I took my place along the barre. She gave me a slight nod before returning her gaze to the next pair.

When we had each done another round of the exercise, Miss Natalia clapped. "I'd like to see all your splits now, please, before we continue." She clasped her hands behind her back and moved to the front of the studio. We all paused for a moment before sinking into our right splits. She moved through our lines as we stretched. I let my stomach rest against my leg and my head fall to the floor. The stretch felt good on my muscles, a gentle pull to release the tension.

Miss Natalia nudged my toe with her foot. "Point. This is not a break." She continued her rounds, observing each of us. "Center splits, please." The process continued. She'd ask for a different split, a different stretch, and then walk around the room. Now and then she'd offer a small correction or a reminder that our muscles should still be engaged.

Miss Natalia clapped to announce the end of class. "There is always so much to do," she said with a small shake of her head. "Have a good evening, girls."

We all rolled out of our stretches and rose to our feet, curtsying to her before collecting our shoes and water bottles. We hadn't even used our pointe shoes today. Outside in the dressing room, we each slipped into our street shoes in silence.

I had just pulled on my shirt and begun to unpin my bun when Miss Natalia called me back into the studio. "Nova, come here, please."

I steeled myself for another lecture. Just when I thought I had been doing better. Miss Natalia sat on the piano bench, her legs crossed and her chin resting in her hands. I stopped in front of her. She studied me for a moment before saying,

"Isaac has told me about you. He sees potential." She played with her gold bangles. "And I must say, if you continue to bring the focus and technique I saw today to class, I agree."

Ten

That night after dinner Beth and I went to the studio. I watched Beth dance and gave corrections. Then we switched. Back and forth, back and forth.

I sat at the front, legs pulled to my chest and chin resting on the remote, watching Beth's jetés. "You're not bending your legs enough before you take off." I reset the music to the beginning of the track. "Makes it so you can't get as much height."

She groaned, her hands braced on her knees while she caught her breath. She'd been practicing her jetés for the better part of an hour, and her leg warmers, shorts, skirt and sweater were scattered around the edges of the studio.

Each marked a point of frustration and over-exertion where she had thrown off another layer.

"I wasn't built for jumps. I'm all about the slow exercises." She wiped sweat from her forehead and moved back to a corner.

"Just plié. It'll help." I pressed *Play*.

Beth made progress across the floor, her movements long and liquid as she moved through the preparatory steps. Her legs weren't quite in a flat split in the jump.

She changed direction and started moving toward the opposite corner.

Another change in direction. Another jeté.

"YES! Beth, that was better."

The music finished, and she collapsed to the floor, legs and arms spread out. "I'm never moving again."

"You're the one who wanted to come."

"Not for death by jetés. For practice."

"This *is* practice."

She sat up and scooted across the floor until she sat beside me, back against the mirror. "All right, then, it's your turn. For fouettés."

I groaned. "Now that's just cruel."

"Up." She flicked her wrist to get me moving. "Just do them on the right side until the music runs out."

I moved to the center of the studio and faced the mirror. Shoulders back and weight forward. The music started, and I did a single turn. *Add the leg next. Right leg to the front, then over to the side, then back into the retiré, so my legs look like a numeral four.* I turned as I moved my leg to the side. Again. I whipped my head around so I didn't get dizzy.

"You're leaning to the right," Beth called.

Lift through my waist to stop leaning. Point my foot. Leg front, side, in.

The music ended. I didn't bother running off to the side like I would have in class, stopping only when I faced the front again, in mid-turn. I bent over, hands on my hips and chest heaving. A stitch had woven its way through my side, and pain shot from it with each breath.

Beth ignored my breathlessness and continued with her corrections. "You need to move as a unit. Coordinate your head, arms and legs so the turn works. Other side."

Six sides later, Beth said my turns had gotten a little better. We decided that was enough for one night. I started untying the ribbon of one of my pointe shoes, picking at the ends to loosen the knot.

I slipped off one shoe and scrunched and unscrunched my toes. "Before I left, everybody kept saying how amazing these weeks would be." I started working on the knot on my second shoe.

Beth played with the battery compartment on the remote. "And they haven't been?"

"There's just all this pressure to have an amazing time—dancing and in the city and I'm..." I glanced up at her. "I'm not sure that I even want to dance professionally."

Beth set the remote aside. "You don't have to decide right now, Nova."

I moved to lie back with my legs up against the mirror, letting the blood drain from my tired and puffy feet. "But I will soon."

"You can always change your mind, do something different."

Feeling began to tingle back into my toes. "What about you? Is this what you want to do?"

"I mean...yeah. This is it for me. The buzz of everything else fades when I'm dancing. It's just me and the music."

"My aunt said it was like that for her too." I'd never talked about Aunt Ivy much with Beth but I took a deep breath and continued. "She has cystic fibrosis. But she would have been this amazing dancer if she didn't."

Beth lay down beside me. She folded her hands across her stomach. "You don't have to dance because she can't, you know," she said gently.

"I know." I swallowed. "But I feel like I should."

Eleven

There was a knock on the door the next morning. Beth walked in, her backpack slung over her shoulder. I sat up, confused. Today was a free day, and we hadn't made any plans. Immy had already taken off. I was so tired I just wanted to sleep all day.

"We," Beth declared, "are going on a picnic." She held up a hand. "No objections. You need to have some fun, Abbott. Let's move it!" Her spiral curls bounced.

"Sir, yes, sir." I jumped to the floor and quickly changed into shorts and a T-shirt. On the way out, I grabbed my sunglasses.

Beth's phone rang just as we got outside the building. "Hello? Mom. Hi."

Beth kept walking but slowed down, paying no attention to the crowds. People pushed past her. A man in a suit knocked into her shoulder. She just managed not to fall off the curb. I grabbed her elbow and pulled her behind me. Left at the camera store. Another left at the end of the block. I held on to Beth until we reached the park. I had managed to navigate us through the crowds.

We selected a sunny patch of grass perfect for people watching. Beth started pulling food out of her backpack. She had come prepared. I plucked a strawberry from the plastic container Beth held out.

I lay back and closed my eyes against the sun. I realized that the bustle of people soothed me now like a familiar lullaby. "I think I like New York."

"You think?" Beth answered, mouth full.

I sat up and reached for another strawberry. "I didn't before, but it's grown on me."

"I'm sure New York would be pleased to know that it has impressed you."

"It's just all gotten better, you know." I licked my fingers. It all had. The classes, the girls, the city. It felt like I fit in now. All the things I loved about ballet were coming back to me. The feeling of freedom when I danced, the emotion that came with each step. Being in a serious class with serious teachers and peers had changed my focus. If I wanted to do this, to make a career out of it, I knew New York was the place I had to be.

"I'm glad," Beth said.

We munched on sandwiches and watched the people going by. A group of joggers, all dressed in bright spandex, with water bottles on their hips. A mother with a stroller, chasing after a toddler on his tricycle. We caught snippets of conversations and tinny music from headphones as everyone moved past.

A group of girls rode by on tandem bikes. Their steering was jerky, and they kept losing their balance. "I've always wanted to try that," I said. I sat up straighter. "Hey, want to right now? We can explore more of the city that way."

Beth rolled over and turned her head so her cheek rested against her arm. "Okay, but you're riding in the front."

I stood up, brushing grass off my legs. "I'm good with that." I felt ready to be the trailblazer.

* * *

Beth and I returned to the dorm that evening tired and sunburned after our adventures around the city. Riding the tandem had been difficult. It had taken us nearly an hour to fall into sync and not tip over every few minutes. But once we had figured it out, we had gone all over New York. We rode by Grand Central Station and the Brooklyn Bridge. We waved to the Statue of Liberty and saw the Empire State Building. My legs ached as I climbed the stairs to my room. When I got there I called my dad. I wanted to tell him and Aunt Ivy all about my great day.

Dad picked up on the third ring. Finally. He had been so hard to reach lately. "Hi, Pop."

"Nova! One second. I'll put you on speaker-phone."

Aunt Ivy this time. "Nova! Tell us...about... the Big...Apple!"

Her voice sounded breathier than usual. Raspy. She coughed a deep, hacking cough.

"You were right—the buildings here are incredible. And Central Park! I'm really starting to love it here."

"And the dancing?" Dad asked.

"The dancing is good—better now."

"It wasn't before?" He sounded surprised.

"Not at first. I missed you guys so much. And some of the girls were messing with my head. But I've been doing some extra practices by myself and with my friend Beth." I stopped while Aunt Ivy coughed. "I feel like it's all fitting into place now."

"You should...have...told us about...your trouble," Aunt Ivy said.

"I needed to figure it out on my own." Even I hadn't realized that until I said it. "So how are you two? I miss you."

Aunt Ivy answered quickly. "Oh, we're...both...fine...just fine. Nothing...to report." But there was something about her super-cheerful voice that made me wonder.

Dad didn't chime in with any of his own news. And there was none of their good-natured arguing. It was like they were both on their best behavior for some reason.

We said our goodbyes. But my hands shook as I set the phone down on my bed. I stared at the black screen. I tried to put my suspicions out of my head. It didn't work. Instead, the worry spread like a finely woven spider web, catching everything in its sticky glue.

I knew everything at home was not fine.

Twelve

After class we all sat on the floor again, taking off our pointe shoes. I filled Beth in on my conversation with Aunt Ivy and Dad from the night before.

"Something's wrong, I'm telling you."

"But they'd tell you if there was a problem, wouldn't they?" She picked at the knot in her ribbon.

"I think they don't want to worry me while I'm here. But now I'm worried anyway and don't even know if there's a reason to be."

"Maybe you're just reading into it."

I slipped off my left pointe shoe. "They were so formal on the phone. And Dad hardly said a word. I know there's something they're not telling me."

"What do you think it is?"

"Well, Aunt Ivy couldn't stop coughing—"

Miss Natalia clapped for our attention. Blood was rushing back into my numbed feet, and my toes tingled with feeling again. I twisted toward her.

"As you know, we only have three days left in the program. Isaac and I have been very impressed with all of you."

It sounded like she was about to make a big announcement. We had all stopped moving. She had our full attention now.

"Tomorrow, Joffrey's artistic director, Ramona Su, and a few company soloists will be observing the class."

Beth and I glanced at each other, our eyebrows raised. Ramona Su was a legend.

But Miss Natalia wasn't done. "I am pleased to tell you that up to three dancers from this program may be offered apprenticeships for the upcoming season. This is a wonderful opportunity that could be the start of your dance career. So I expect all of you to dance your best."

Her eyes ran across the room, pausing briefly on each one of us. "That will be all." She turned to the CD player and began organizing the music.

We all sat there, shocked. Immy broke the silence when she grabbed her pointe shoes and the hard plaster clattered against the floor. Harriet followed, falling into step beside Immy on the way out. Immy's squeal could be heard from the foyer. "Oh. My. Goodness. This is it, Harriet! My big break."

The rest of us gathered our things, hurried whispers floating along the line.

Miss Natalia called Beth and me back. She waited until the door had swung closed before speaking. "I have high hopes for you two tomorrow. You must dance your best." She raised a single eyebrow and then nodded at the door. We were dismissed.

"Okay. Okay." Beth waited until we were out on the sidewalk before grabbing my arm. "Okay. So that just happened."

I was still in shock. "They like us!"

"They *really* like us," Beth corrected.

"We have to practice tonight."

"We have to practice *a lot* tonight," Beth said.

"We can do this?" It came out as a question.

"We can do this," Beth said.

We started walking back to the dorm, crossing the street when it was clear instead of waiting for the pedestrian light. Like true New Yorkers. I picked at my nails while we walked, blood budding against my skin.

Beth linked her arm through mine. I dropped my hand. "It's all going to be okay," she said. "We'll be ready for tomorrow, and you'll call your dad, and it'll all be okay."

I brushed at the red that spread onto my nail and focused on keeping in step with her. I started chewing my lip. I couldn't decide if I was more worried about class the next day or Aunt Ivy.

Thirteen

"Lift your knee as you extend your leg, Nova." Beth sat on the piano bench at the front of the studio. I tried again, glancing at the mirror while I held my leg out behind me. Her trick worked. My foot was higher this time, in line with my shoulder.

"Your hip is up," she called.

"Picky, picky." But she was right. I focused on lowering my hip while still keeping my leg high.

"Admit it," Beth said. The music ended. "You'd be lost without me."

"You're very wise," I said.

She ignored my sarcasm. "Thank you for finally acknowledging that. Now is there anything else you want to work on for tomorrow?"

I glanced at the clock. Almost nine thirty. We had been here since six thirty. But no matter what, it wouldn't be enough practice. "I thought I'd put on my new pair of pointe shoes to break them in a little." The pair I had been wearing for most of the program had become too soft in class earlier that day. The once-hard plaster of the box caved under my thumb when I pressed it. All the pressure and sweat had broken it down.

Beth slid onto the floor and into her splits. "I'll stretch while you do that then. But we should be going soon. Curfew and all."

I sat down and slipped on both shoes, wrapping the ribbons carefully around my ankle. We hadn't turned the main lights on. Now that it was getting dark out, the one safety light shone in the corner, casting a soft glow on Beth. The studio felt calm with just the two of us, reassuring. I could almost feel the tension leaving my body, the worry of my mind settling.

"You nervous?"

Beth lifted her head, propping her chin in her palm as she considered. "Not nervous, really. More jittery, you know?"

My stomach fluttered in response. But, like Beth, I knew it was more out of excitement than nerves. I stood and went on pointe, testing my new shoes. The soles arched perfectly beneath my feet, and I couldn't feel the floor through the box. I took the barre again, the wood cool and smooth beneath my hands, and rolled back up onto full pointe.

Beth flopped out of her stretch and onto her back. "If I don't move, I'm going to fall asleep."

I continued with my rises but hummed in agreement. "We should get a good night's sleep."

"Big day tomorrow."

"Big day tomorrow," I agreed.

I took off my pointe shoes and slipped back into my street clothes. We both thanked the security guard as we left, waving to her as she locked the door behind us. Beth linked her arm through mine and we made our way back to the dorm in comfortable silence. The daytime bustle of the city had calmed down along with the blistering temperatures. Just before we went inside, I paused and looked up at the cloudless black sky. The moon was out now, big and bright and almost full.

I traced the constellations above, though they weren't as easy to spot in the brightness of the city. Just then a star shot across the sky, a bold and brilliant streak in the otherwise quiet night. I released a breath I hadn't been aware I was holding. It felt like a sign from Dad, like we were side by side at the quarry, looking up at the sky. I could feel the cliff rock pressing against my spine. I could hear his voice. *You can do this, kiddo.*

Beth nudged me gently. "Nova? Ready to go in?"

I glanced over at her. "Yeah. I'm ready."

When we reached the third floor, Beth gave me a tired wave and headed up the stairs to her room.

"Hey, want to meet early tomorrow to stretch and warm up for class?" I called to her.

She leaned over the handrail to reply. "Seven thirty in the lobby?"

"Perfect." I pushed through the door to my floor, pulled out my cell and called Dad. Nothing. I dialed again. "Pick up, pick up, pick up, pick up," I muttered. There was a click on the other end of the line.

"Nova?" Dad's voice was heavy, slow.

"Hey, Dad. Did I wake you up? I know it's late."

"No, no, I was up. I'm actually—" He stopped. Muffled sounds in the background. His voice was louder when he spoke again. "What's up? Everything okay?"

"The artistic director is coming to the class tomorrow to scout apprentices!"

There was more muffled noise in the background. I heard what sounded like an announcement over an intercom.

"Dad, what's going on? Where are you?"

I asked the question even though I knew the answer. I knew those sounds. Doctors in starched coats and bright sneakers running back and forth. People in wheelchairs and on beds in halls, waiting for surgery, recovering from surgery, hoping to recover.

I sank to the floor outside my door, suddenly unable to stand. The wall pressed uncomfortably into my spine, and my ear burned against the phone. Neither Dad nor I spoke. Our silence was filled in by the intercom announcements and conversations that leaked from his side of the phone.

Finally he said, "It's Ivy." I closed my eyes, willing him to stop. "She's in the hospital. She has pneumonia. The doctors have her on antibiotics and fluids. She's asleep right now." His voice lowered. "Nova? You still there?"

I picked at a loose thread on my leggings, winding it around my finger until the tip turned white. I unwound the thread and then rewrapped it. "Should I come home?" I asked quietly.

"Soon. You can stay in New York until the end of the program if you want, or come back now. Say the word and I'll book you a flight home whenever."

"Okay" was all I could manage.

"Okay," he said in return.

We stayed on the phone for a few minutes longer, not speaking but comforting each other with our connection.

Finally my dad broke the silence. "I should go check on her," he said. "We'll talk soon, kiddo."

"Talk soon," I echoed. He clicked off, and then I was alone in the hallway. I tried to focus on the numb tingling that had begun in my feet. My hands were shaking. I pictured Aunt Ivy small in a hospital bed, her curly hair like roots, tangled and ungroomed and wild around her head. Roots to anchor her to the world, to us, to Dad and me. Because she couldn't leave. She just couldn't.

I took a deep breath that I felt in my ribs. It seemed cruel that I could breathe such deep, full breaths without thinking while Aunt Ivy fought for each one of hers. I was able to breathe through the pain rippling along my chest. I thought of the audition the next day, of the hours on hours of ballet classes that had brought me here, to this moment, to tomorrow. Everything had all led up to now.

And then I thought of Aunt Ivy. Aunt Ivy who had given me so much. Who had helped me get here. I had to be there for her.

I needed to be in both places. I let that deep breath out. Dad had said it was up to me to decide. But how could I choose between ballet and Aunt Ivy?

Fourteen

When I could finally, finally get off the floor and go into my room, I slid out of my shoes and crawled right into bed. Brushing my teeth, washing my face and changing out of my leotard and tights required more energy than I had. Even the sheet felt like too much pressure against my skin. I lay on my side, my head cushioned in the crook of my arm, watching the curtain rustle. The breeze that blew through the open window was the only relief from the stuffy room.

While Immy snored away, I faded in and out of sleep, restless and uncomfortable. The image of Aunt Ivy in a hospital bed met me each time I closed my eyes. At 3:00 AM I checked my phone for what felt like the hundredth time. Nothing. No updates, no missed calls. I rummaged in my suitcase for the ring I had bought for Aunt Ivy. I turned it over in my hands, tracing the silver swirls of wire. The man in the store had said the endless knot represented beginnings and endings.

Today, this class, this was it. My opportunity. My chance to see if I had it in me to be a professional ballerina—if I had that spark and drive that allowed them to dance all day, every day, to train and perform night after night. To dedicate my life to this art.

"She knows I have to do this." My voice came out in a whisper. For a moment I wasn't sure who had spoken. I slipped the ring onto my finger. There. It was a relief to have it out—to acknowledge that I had to do it, for myself but also for Aunt Ivy. I couldn't count all the times she had sat middle-center at my performances. All the pirouettes she'd watched me do in the kitchen. All the pointe shoes she'd sewn ribbons on over the years.

Now that I had made up my mind, I didn't waste any time. Grabbing my laptop, I searched for flights and texted my dad the information.

With any luck I'd be home and with Aunt Ivy before midnight. All I could hope was that I wouldn't be too late.

*　*　*

Beth and I walked over to the studio together. I wasn't in the mood to talk. She left me to my silence as I pinned her number to the front and back of her bodysuit. The whole room was quiet. Girls touched up their hair with hairspray or stretched by themselves, their eyes distant. Today was a big day.

When it came time for class to start, we fell into line according to the numbers we'd been assigned. Beth and I were five and six. Beth inhaled sharply when Isaac opened the studio door.

"Okay, girls, we're ready for you now," he said.

As we filed in, Beth grabbed my hand and whispered, "Break a leg." I squeezed her hand, my throat too tight to respond. Aunt Ivy's ring dug into my finger.

My nerves tingled for both me and Aunt Ivy. I decided to try and file away every detail of the class so I could give her a play-by-play later. She'd want to know. When she woke up.

"Oh my god, there she is!" whispered Beth.

Five people sat in a line along the front of the room. Ramona Su sat in the center. I recognized her from the school's brochure and videos I'd watched online of her dancing. She sat with her ankles neatly crossed and her back straight. Miss Natalia sat beside her, her hair in a French twist again and a clipboard in her lap. The other three, a man and two women, sat on either side of them, eyes on us as we filed in. It was clear they were dancers too, even though they weren't moving. A pianist sat at the piano, her hands folded and her feet resting on the pedals. The fan already whirred in the corner, a cool breeze ruffling against our skin.

Isaac clapped his hands. "This is it, ladies. Show us your best—let's start with pliés."

Isaac moved in a blur as he demonstrated each exercise. I watched but had trouble taking in what he was doing. I couldn't translate his movements to my body, to achieve the coordination of my muscles, my legs and arms. My balance was off when I rose onto demi-pointe.

I fell backward and was just able to grab the barre to keep myself from falling over.

With each exercise, when I glanced over to check my placement, the mirror seemed to reflect images of Aunt Ivy. Spinning on the lawn with her head thrown back. Sewing pointe shoes in the dressing room while she waited for me to finish class. Applying my stage makeup before I learned to do it myself. She was always there.

Then I'd glimpse the row of examiners with their clipboards. Their eyes scanned the line, pausing briefly on each girl before they made a note and continued down the line.

Suddenly my foot cramped, a sharp and definite pain that anchored me in the studio. I focused on Beth in front of me. On the gold safety pins that fastened her number to her leotard. The blue scrunchie around her bun. I unfolded my leg behind me. My back muscles shook, and I could feel my leg dropping no matter how I fought it.

And then, thankfully, the piano stopped, and we all lowered our legs and breathed a collective sigh of relief.

Isaac called, "All right, ladies, stretch and then we'll move into the center."

The examiners leaned forward in their chairs. Their heads almost touched as they whispered, their voices too soft and far away for us to catch. Beth turned to me and raised an eyebrow. I knew she was asking how it was going. I shook my head slightly in response—*not well.* She smiled and gave me a thumbs-up and mouthed *You got this.*

I turned to the barre and stretched my calves. I focused on the pull of muscle rippling along my leg and the prickle of heat on my skin. The fan wasn't doing much to cool the room. I ran my hands along the smooth grain of the barre. There were patches of heat where I had held it throughout the exercises.

Aunt Ivy's ring tapped against the wood. I closed my eyes and pressed further into the stretch. I imagined myself in the studio alone. Just me and the music, propelling myself forward, working through the steps. Dancing in Aunt Ivy's backyard in the bright spring air, the sun along my back and my feet cushioned by grass. Just dancing, moving through the movements for my own sake and not anybody else's. Aunt Ivy sitting on the porch behind me, clapping to music that wasn't there.

I opened my eyes again. This time the teachers didn't seem so intimidating, and the lights weren't quite as harsh. I sighed quietly and sank down into the splits. Maybe I could do this after all.

Isaac moved to the front of the room and held up his hand for our attention. "Ladies! Let's begin again."

I focused on my own steps, the feel of the floor beneath my feet, solid and *there*. It would catch me if I fell.

In posé pirouettes, I imagined myself as a ballerina in a music box, turning, turning, turning like it was nothing, the easiest thing in the world. I was only vaguely aware of Beth beside me, spinning in time with the music, our movements in sync. *Back straight, weight forward, whip my head around.* A perfect triple. Delight tingled down my spine, a zing of pride. *Shoulders down, pointed foot, stick the landing.*

Beth poked me in the back when we finished the exercise and ran off to the side to let the next pair go. "Immy doesn't know what she has coming."

I stopped myself from looking around to find Immy. No doubt she was showing off her perfect positions at the barre. I didn't need to intimidate myself. I had done a perfect triple. I could do this.

When the last pair had finished, we all merged back into our lines for jumps. Plié, I reminded myself, remember to plié. When I fell behind the music I corrected myself. Not *too* much plié. I felt weightless as we traveled across the floor. My cheeks were warm, and sweat darkened my bodysuit, but I no longer felt uncomfortable in the heat.

The exercise ended, and I took a long drink from my water bottle. Isaac spoke with the panel at the front. He nodded at them and then moved back toward us. "We'll finish with grand jetés. One at a time, in a zigzag across the floor. Numerical order, please." We all shuffled into line. He nodded at the pianist. "And..."

She began playing, the melody reaching the corners of the room and overtaking all of us. Immy went first. Her splits were flat in her grand jeté, perfect execution. She changed direction, and the second girl went. She stumbled slightly before her jump, her feet caught beneath her.

We peeled off from our line at the barre one by one, each falling into step with the girl before. One girl zigged when the other zagged. Beth next, her back long and straight as she prepared. She began her steps and launched into a jeté, her front leg unfolding into a perfect line. She seemed to stay there, suspended in the air.

My turn. I stretched my right leg out in preparation and then moved across the floor, low and grounded so I could push off and get height. Arms extended, I reached out of my shoulders and past the studios like I could fly to Aunt Ivy. I landed in a plié and carried my leg over to switch directions and start my zag. I sailed through the air.

Another zig, another zag, and then I ran off to the side, taking my place alongside Beth. My chest heaved. I wiped sweat from my forehead. Beth grabbed my hand and gave it a slight squeeze. *We're done—we can relax.*

When we all stood along the barre, Isaac took a step forward. "That's all for today, girls. Well done. We've got some hard choices to make, but you'll know our decisions by tomorrow."

For a moment none of us moved. Then we collected our water bottles and filed toward the door. Our pointe shoes tapped a staccato rhythm against the hardwood.

It was out of my hands. I had done my best. All I could do now was wait for their decision. In the meantime, I had a plane to catch.

Fifteen

I had left my suitcase in the dressing room during the audition. Now all I had to do was get to the airport. My flight left in three hours. I'd be with Aunt Ivy by eight.

Beth sat beside me on a bench as I struggled into my street clothes. My jeans stuck to my tights, and I jumped around the room to get them on. "Have you heard anything more from your dad?"

"No," I said, slipping my shirt on. He had sent me an email with flight confirmation details but no news on how Aunt Ivy was doing.

She played with the nozzle on her water bottle. "But no news is good news, right?"

I stuffed my pointe shoes into my bag. "Right." I hoped.

"I'm sure your dad would have told you if something had happened."

I hoped she was right.

We walked outside together. She hugged me. "Call me when you know more."

I squeezed her back, her skin sticky with sweat. I couldn't find the words to respond to her or even say a proper goodbye. The weight of what we had just done and where I was going were heavy on my mind.

When we broke apart, I moved to the curb with my arm in the air. I didn't recognize this Nova, so confident and bold. So different from the one who had first come to New York. A taxi pulled up.

"To JFK, please," I said to the driver when I slid into the back seat. We sped away, weaving through traffic, just one more cab in the buzz of the city. I watched the buildings blur together. I checked my phone. No messages. Dad's phone went straight to voice mail when I called.

I left a message. "Hi, Dad, it's me. Just letting you know I'm headed to the airport now. I'll grab a taxi when I land and meet you at the hospital. Okay? Bye."

I closed my eyes after I hung up, trying not to think about what his silence meant.

I only hoped I wasn't too late.

Sixteen

This hospital looked like every other one Aunt Ivy had been in over the years. White floors blended into white walls. Bright paintings were meant to look cheerful. Nurses bustled about in colorful scrubs, and doctors in white lab coats consulted charts. The smell of cleaning products hung in the air.

I burst through the automatic doors and went straight to the main desk. A nurse with a yellow stethoscope around his neck sat at the computer. He looked up as I approached.

My suitcase crashed against my ankles. "I'm here to see a patient named Ivy Abbott?" Half question, half statement.

"Are you family?"

"I'm her niece."

The keyboard clattered as he typed. "Unit 8, room 52."

"Right, thanks." I turned, paused.

"Sixth floor," he said.

A man with white hair and a cane waited at the elevator. He wore a suit and a red bow tie and carried a bouquet of flowers and a book. I suddenly felt unprepared. I had come empty-handed, sweat still caked on my skin from class, and tights itching beneath my jeans. The elevator dinged, and we both stepped inside. He pressed the button for floor twelve, his eyes heavy. My panic mounted as we rose.

"Room 52, 52, 52," I repeated under my breath as I made my way down the hallway, peering through each door. Finally I spotted Dad, stretched out in the chair beside Aunt Ivy's bed. He jumped when I touched his shoulder.

"Nova." He stood and wrapped me in a hug, his cheek resting against my hair.

I leaned back. "You look tired." Stubble ran along his jaw and made the dark circles under his eyes more obvious. His shirt was wrinkled and the top button was undone.

"It's been a long couple of days," he replied, voice quiet. He stepped back to give me a view of Aunt Ivy. "She's unconscious. They're not sure when she'll wake up."

I took Dad's hand as I looked at her—the white sheets and hospital gown made her look pale. Her hair was wrapped around her head in snarls of brown. An oxygen mask was strapped to her face, and IVs were buried in her arm.

"She has to wake up."

"I know." He squeezed my shoulder.

I turned to him. "You should eat, change. I'll stay with her." He massaged his temples. "I'll call you if the doctor comes in."

He exhaled. "Okay."

"Okay," I repeated, because there was nothing more to say.

I took Dad's place beside her. The chair cushion was worn and uncomfortable. Too many people had sat there before me, waiting.

I took Aunt Ivy's hand in mine, tracing the lengths of her fingers and knuckles. Her skin was chilled from the air conditioning in the room. "I had an audition today, at Joffrey. The company is going to take on some apprentices from the summer camp." It felt right to talk to her. She was always who I wanted to share my news with first. The good and the bad. And this was big, maybe the first big move of my career.

"It's been hard. The classes, the competition with the other girls. The teachers all know what they're talking about and want you to do it right every time." A pause. "But it's felt good, once I stopped being hung up on the technical aspects of it—and how I compared to the other girls. As soon as I let go, it went better."

A nurse came in just then. "Excuse me, honey, I'm just going to take her vitals."

I let go of Aunt Ivy's hand. "When will she wake up?"

The nurse listened to Aunt Ivy's shallow breaths with a stethoscope. "We've just got to wait and see. Her breathing isn't great, but she's on antibiotics. It's hard. The CF makes the pneumonia worse than it would usually be." She took Aunt Ivy's temperature.

"Yeah." This wasn't the first time we had camped out next to Aunt Ivy's hospital bed.

The nurse recorded the results of her tests in the chart. "She's tough. Don't give up yet."

"She always has been a fighter." I said this to the nurse's back as she left to tend to other patients.

I scooted my chair closer to Aunt Ivy's bed, taking her hand in both of mine to warm it. "They said they were really interested in me especially. Me and Beth, my friend from Vancouver. That felt like added pressure, walking into the studio at the beginning of class today. Knowing they were paying closer attention—"

"Knock, knock."

I turned. Dad came in. He still wore the same rumpled clothes but carried a paper coffee cup in each hand. "Coffee, no sugar and lots of milk."

I took the offered cup and sipped. The liquid burned when I swallowed, tracing a path down my throat. It wasn't quite coffee, but it would do. "The nurse just checked on her."

Dad nodded, settling in the chair on the other side of the bed. He glanced at his watch. "Someone usually comes in around this time."

"Right."

"How did it go then? You said there was an audition?"

"Yeah, to become an apprentice in the company."

He leaned closer. "Nova, that's an amazing opportunity. I'm so proud of you."

"I haven't gotten it yet." I glanced over at Aunt Ivy, tapping my cup. I still wore her ring and the sound it made against the cup was reassuring. I slipped it off and onto one of her fingers, pushing it past the knuckle.

"From New York, Aunt Ivy."

"She'd be so happy, Nova," Dad said quietly. "She really would."

I swallowed. I already knew how happy she would be, how proud.

*　　*　　*

By morning Aunt Ivy's breathing had changed. Now it was ragged, shallow, short. She lay still in the bed, bathed in sunlight. The peonies Dad had brought in earlier were beginning to droop, and a few of the large pink petals were sprinkled around the base of the vase.

Our world had shifted, grown smaller. We were entirely focused on Aunt Ivy. But everything else remained the same. The sun still shone into the room, and birds chirped in the trees outside.

My empty coffee cup sat on the table beside me, along with a chocolate bar I couldn't bring myself to eat.

Dad and I pressed closer to her, powerless. I wove my fingers with hers. The light shone on the blue stone of her ring. Every few minutes one of us whispered, "We love you, Ivy."

When my phone rang, a soft vibration in my pocket, I answered it automatically. Beth.

She didn't wait for me to answer, talking as soon as the call connected. "We got it!"

I couldn't quite place her voice or her news in my new surroundings. My ears buzzed. "What?"

"You and me."

I didn't respond.

"The apprenticeships?"

I sat up straighter, the hospital chair digging into my back. "They want us?"

"Both of us. Isaac said you can give them an answer within the week. To not worry about it and just focus on being with your family right now. But we got it."

I listened to Aunt Ivy's uneven breathing. She had been born to be a dancer. She moved like a willow, delicately blown by the breeze. The only thing that had kept her tethered to the ground was her oxygen tank.

Without thinking I replied. "Can you tell Isaac yes for me?"

I would dance beneath the stage lights for her. This would be for both of us.

Acknowledgments

First, always, thank you to my family, my parents, Dianne and David, and my brother, Matthew, for your support and encouragement in everything I do. Thanks for being in the audience at fourteen years' worth of *The Nutcracker* and *Etudé* performances and cheering every time. And thanks, Mom, for the hundreds of hours you volunteered in wardrobe and backstage.

And thank you to everyone at Orca, especially Andrew and Ruth, for giving me the opportunity to be both a member of the team and a published writer, and Tanya, for guiding me through this process. I'm grateful for everything.

KATHERINE RICHARDS has an MA in Creative Writing from Bath Spa University in the UK. She trained in classical ballet at the International School of Ballet for fourteen years, dancing in productions such as *The Nutcracker*, *Les Sylphides* and *Coppélia*. *Nova in New York* is her first novel. For more information, visit katherinerichards.ca.